Little Wolf and Smellybreff

What's the Time, Little Wolf?

Ian Whybrow + Tony Ross

HarperCollins *Children's Books*

In a nice smelly lair, far away, lived the Wolf family.
They were all bad except for Little Wolf, and he
tried his hardest not to be good.
One day, not long before dinner time, he was painting.
His baby brother was playing with his little drill and chopper.

"Stop it, Smells!" said
Little Wolf. "Now you've
made me do a smudge."

"Ow-wooooooo!"
howled Smellybreff.

"Gurr!" said Dad.
"Too noisy!
Go outside
and play!"

"Go on, Little," said Mum. "Take your baby brother
and catch a nice, fat piggy for dinner."
"But Mum," said Little. "The piggies' house is
miles away and you know Smells
will keep moaning and asking what time it is."

"Out!" gurred Dad. "And
don't come back with
an empty sack!"

Little was right.
As soon as they were
out of the gate,
Smellybreff started.

"I'm hungry!" he moaned.
"When will we catch a piggy?"

"In a
MINUTE!"
said Little.

And when they reached
the lake, Smells was
still being a pain.

"I'm hungry!" he whined. "What's the time, Little Wolf?"

Just at that moment, Little spied a nest full of chicks.

"It's chicks o'clock!" he smiled.

"Time to catch some chicks for dinner!

We'll huff and we'll puff and we'll BLOW their nest down!"

But Smells didn't want to huff and puff. He wanted to chop with his little chopper.

"Look out, chicks!" he shouted. "I will hop, I will plop, I will CHOP your house down!"

SPLASH!

went the chicks' nest,
into the lake.

"Ow-wooooo!" howled
Little Wolf and Smells.
"Now we're all wet and no
dinner in the sack!"

So on they went until Little spied some bees.
"I'm **HUNGRY!**" whined Smells. "What's the time, Little Wolf?"
Little Wolf said, "Don't worry, it's bee o'clock.
Time to collect some honey for dinner!

We'll huff and
we'll puff and
we'll BLOW their
hive down!"

But Smellybreff didn't
want to huff and puff.
He wanted to drill with
his little drill.

"Look out, bees!"
he shouted. "I will hill,
I will pill, I will DRILL
your house down!"

"Ow-woooooo!" howled Little Wolf and Smells.
"Now we're all wet and stung and STILL
no dinner in the sack!"

On they went,
tired and hungry...

until **AT LAST**...

...they reached
the piggies' house.

How the piggies laughed!
They sang:

"You two weakies can't get in,
Not by the hair on your chinny-chin-chin!"

Poor Little Wolf! He did his best by huffing and puffing.
And Smellybreff did his best by drilling and chopping.
But they COULD NOT get in –
not by the hair on their chinny-chin-chin!

That did it.

Smells had a tantrum.

He howled,
"What's the time,
Little Wolf?

What's the time,
Little Wolf?

What's
the time,
Little Wolf?"

Just then, up popped lots of
nosy mice and rabbits.
"We like this game!" they
squeaked. "Can we play?"

"What a good idea!" said Little. "We'll stand here and cover our eyes. You have to wiggle up behind us VERY QUIETLY."

So the nosy mice and rabbits
wiggled up behind Little and Smells.

"What's the time,
Little Wolf?"
they wiggled.

"Fun o'clock!"
whispered Little
to Smells.

"What's the time,
Little Wolf?"
they jiggled.

"Chew o'clock,"
whispered Little.

"What's the time,
Little Wolf?"
they giggled.

"Dinner time!"

shouted Little Wolf and Smells together.

And quick as a chick, their empty sack was FULL.

Dad was in a very good temper that evening.
"Lovely mice pies, Little!" he said.
"And fine rabbit rolls!" cooed Mum.
"Now tell me, was Smells a VERY bad cub today?"

"Very bad!" laughed Little.
"And, thank badness, he never stopped
moaning and asking me what the time was...

...yum, yum!"